The Magic in the Mirror

To Emily,
Dream beyond your
wildest dreams!!!
much love,
April

Written by

April Bernardi & Carol Baschnagel

Illustrated by

Rick Reason

Edited by Jennifer Baschnagel

DEAR READERS

First let me congratulate you on your choice to pick up this

magical book. You may not know it yet, but in your choice you

are about to go on an adventure of discovery like you have

never done before. You will learn great secrets that many adults

have yet to become aware of. You will learn about magic, creation,

and creating magic in your own life. And last but not least, you

will learn about the magic in the mirror and how you can use this

magic to turn your own dreams into reality. So now let us meet

Gabriella and see how she learned all about the magic in the mirror.

The story of Gabriella begins when she was one year old. It was at this age that she learned to walk. From that moment on, Gabriella never wanted to be held or carrried. She wanted to walk on her own two feet because she loved the feeling of being free: free to discover, free to learn, free to explore the world, and most of all free to use her imagination to create fun things to do.

When Gabriella was two years old, her baby brother Michael was born. Everyone was so happy especially Gabriella. She liked to hold him, feed him, and do anything else that helped her mother with him. She loved being a big sister.

At this time the family lived in a small apartment, but their dream was to one day own a house of their own. Gabriella's parents knew that they could create anything. They knew how to make their dreams come true. They knew that once they saved enough money, they would create a beautiful home for their family to live in by using their imaginations. So they set a picture in their minds of what this house would look like. Next they imagined how they would feel once they finished the house. Then they set their goal and began to create their vision.

inally when Gabriella turned three years old, their dream came true. They bought their first house. Oh how happy they all were! Gabriella could barely wait to see it.

A few days later, when the family pulled their car up to the new house, Gabriella blinked her eyes several times. This couldn't be the house they waited to buy for so long. It was the ugliest house she had ever seen! Her parents started to laugh for they knew what Gabriella was thinking. However, they assured her that this was their house and that by the time they were done, it was going to be exactly as they had envisioned it. Gabriella was skeptical, but she tried to be positive since she didn't want to hurt her parents' feelings.

The next day, the family got to work on creating their vision. Everyone had a job to do by using his or her talents. Gabriella's mother was a talented decorator. She had a passion for decorating. A passion is doing something you love to do. With her decorating skills, Gabriella's mother could totally transform an otherwise boring room into a spectacular and inviting one. Gabriella's father also had a passion, which was to fix or build things. He was a talented carpenter. Using their gifts and combining their efforts, the parents went to work on the house. The first thing they did was rent a dumpster to dispose of all the garbage that was left in the house from the original owners.

They decided to sand and paint some of the old furniture, making it look like new. One item that Gabriella especially liked was an old milk box made out of wood. She and her mother painted it white with pink flowers. They then lined the inside with pink and white wallpaper. When they finished, Gabriella used it as a treasure chest to store all of her most prized possessions. Soon the house was emptied of all the clutter, and it was time to clean. Gabriella and her mother went to the store to buy all sorts of cleaning products. Gabriella had her own little mop and broom; she loved working beside her mom. It felt like they were playing house all day long.

After the house was cleaned, they began to paint the walls. This was the most fun of all. Gabriella loved the smell of fresh paint. It made the house smell new. She enjoyed helping to select the different colors for each room. After the house was painted, Gabriella began to see her parents' vision unfold as the old ugly house began to transform before her very eyes.

Gabriella's favorite room in the whole house was her room. When it came time to decorate her bedroom, Gabriella was able to incorporate all of her own ideas. Together, the family created a beautiful room that Gabriella called "paradise" and her mother called "heaven on earth." The room had a high ceiling, which made Gabriella feel free. The ceiling was painted to look like the sky. It was aquamarine with white fluffy clouds and a huge sun in the corner. A colorful rainbow was in the other corner, which made Gabriella feel happy. It was truly a wonderful sight to begin each day. On one wall, her mother painted a huge tree with green leaves and brown branches. It looked so real. It made Gabriella feel like she was connected to nature and to the earth. At the foot of the tree were flowers, grass, ducks, and a pretty sunflower that made Gabriella feel loved.

Gabriella's bed was also very unique. Her father constructed her bed into a giant dollhouse. It had a door, a window, and it was big enough for all of Gabriella's friends to lie in. She added a play stove and refrigerator to the inside, and her mattress was on the top of this house. This room also contained a loft. Her father built a staircase that led up to the top of the loft so the children could get up to it. It was here that Gabriella, Michael, and their friends held secret meetings. Gabriella loved her room so much because she felt safe and warm here. But more importantly she felt that she had created her room with her own imagination. That made her feel proud.

Gabriella felt like the luckiest girl in the world because she had learned the secret of creation. First you have a vision. Then you try to paint a picture in your mind of that vision becoming real. Then you use your imagination and let yourself feel what it will be like to create your vision. Soon your vision will become reality.

$\mathcal{F}$inally, the work of creating was finished, and it was time for the family to move into their new home. On the first night that Gabriella slept in her new room and every night thereafter, her mother would come to tuck her in and say goodnight. She would tell Gabriella short stories while Gabriella closed her eyes. Although the stories were always different, they were always reminders of how special Gabriella and every other child in the world is. Her mother would begin by gently pushing the hair back from Gabriella's forehead and while speaking in a soft voice she would say:

Turn on your CD now
and listen along to the
guided meditation or
continue reading.

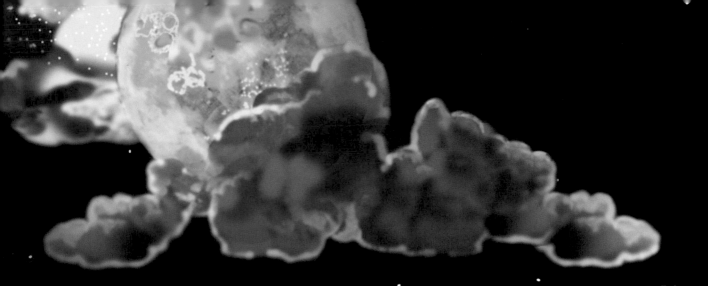

*C*lose your eyes and try to relax. I want
you to imagine something:

Imagine that the ceiling above your bed is opening.
As you look through, you can see the midnight sky
filled with millions and millions of twinkling stars.
Right in the center of the sky, above your bed,
is the brightest, fullest moon you have ever seen.

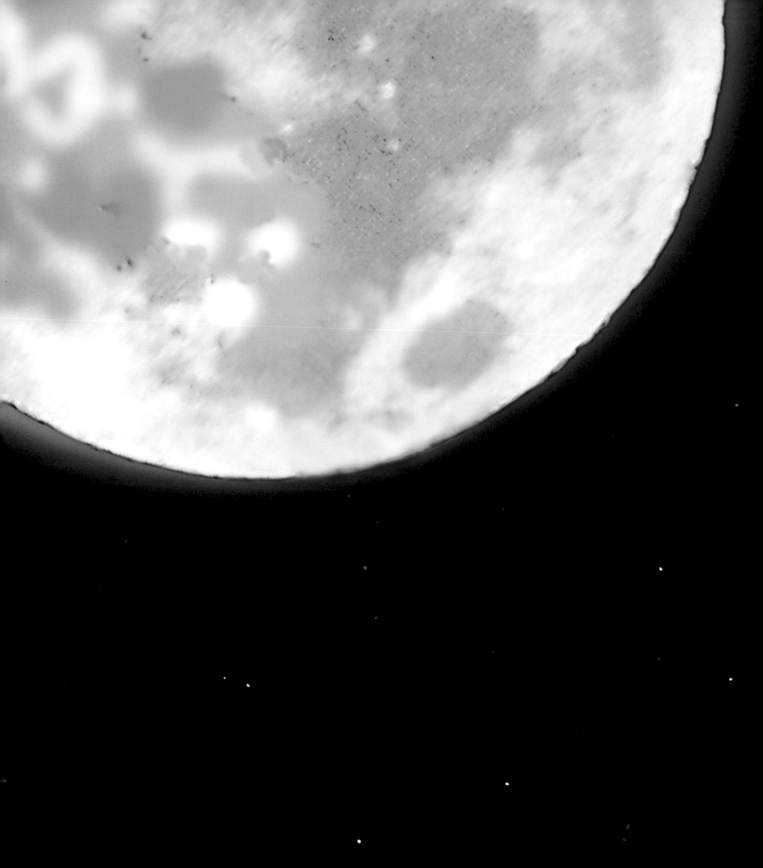

*I*t looks like a white cloud floating lazily by. As you lie in your bed, you can feel the soothing warm light of the moon shining down on you. It has the power to help you feel very relaxed and calm.

Feel this energy now. Feel it enter your body, beginning from the top of your head, the part that was soft when you were a baby and the part where you soul entered your body just before you were born.

Feel this warm energy fill you up right now. It is filling your forehead, eyes, cheeks, lips, mouth, and tongue. As it fills each part, you are feeling more and more peaceful.

It continues to fill your ears, jaw, and chin. It feels so good as it travels down your neck and into your shoulders. Feel your neck and shoulders relax now with this moon energy. Feel how it is moving into your arms, forearms, wrists, and palms of your hands, into your fingers, and finally into each fingertip.

Now it is going to fill up your body, starting with your chest and moving all around your beautiful open heart.

Connect with your heart for a moment. Your heart is what allows you to give and receive love. It provides you with courage and helps you overcome your fears. Feel this courage now. You have the ability to do anything. Everything feels so easy!

Now the moon energy is moving down your spine and into each rib. All your internal organs are filling up, down your belly, and around your belly button.

You feel happy!

Your hips begin to loosen up. It is now traveling into each leg, beginning at the top and moving down in a spiral, around your knees and kneecaps, into your calves and shins.

Peace is filling you like never before. You feel it in your ankles, down your heels, the arches of your feet, and out your toes.

As you lie here, filled with this moon energy, you are feeling lighter and lighter. Your body begins to feel weightless. Like a feather, you start to rise up from your bed and move toward the stars. You are heading for the moon, to the place where all your dreams come true.

Floating through the midnight sky, you see a few birds pass you by. You open your arms and soar even higher through the clouds.

All around you, there is stillness, an incredible sense of calm.

The sky seems brighter now; maybe it is because you are closer to the moon and the source of all creation.

*S*uddenly, far off you see a shining, white light flicker. "Hmmm," you wonder, "what is it?"

You decide to go check it out and quickly but effortlessly you move toward the shining object. You move past the stars and planets. The closer you get, the more quickly you move. You are excited because you feel like you are getting closer to home. It is a familiar feeling that you have experienced before. The feeling like there is no place like home.

Finally you see a very shiny round object floating in the center of the universe. It looks like a mirror. This big round object has a white light radiating from behind it.

You begin to approach the mirror, and as you arrive you see someone standing in it.

IT IS YOU!

As you stare into your own eyes, you are filled with the knowledge that everything you have ever wanted, you already have. You are perfect just as you are.

You now know that you have the power to create anything just by feeling it inside of yourself. You just need to feel the connection to everything. You begin to realize that you are not alone but instead a part of everything and everyone else here on this planet. Everyone came here to share his or her gifts with the rest of the world. By doing this, we are all a part of creation.

*T*his awareness is making you feel empowered because you now know that all you have to do is look inside of yourself for the answers to creating your dreams. You can create your own heaven on earth.

How does this new awareness make you feel? Peaceful? Calm?

Does your heart feel warm and open?

Can you share this feeling with others?

As you float back to lie in your cozy bed, you begin to wonder, "What can I create? What can I share with the world?"

So now you know the secret of the magic in the mirror:
YOU ARE THE MAGIC IN THE MIRROR!
Sweet dreams, Child!

Good Night.